This book belongs to:

. . . .

For Lois Linker – F.W.

To My Grandchildren – H.M.S.

For my friend Gema and her big family – E.O.

JP

This paperback edition first published in 2009 by Andersen Press Ltd.
First published in Great Britain in 2008 by Andersen Press Ltd.,
20 Vauxhall Bridge Road, London SW1V 2SA.
Published in Australia by Random House Australia Pty.,
Level 3, 100 Pacific Highway, North Sydney, NSW 2060.
Text copyright © Ferida Wolff/Harriet May Savitz, 2008.
Illustration copyright © Elena Odriozola, 2008.
The rights of Ferida Wolff, Harriet May Savitz
and Elena Odriozola to be identified as the authors
and illustrator of this work have been asserted by them in
accordance with the Copyright, Designs and Patents Act, 1988.
All rights reserved.

Colour separated in Switzerland by Photolitho AG, Zürich.
Printed and bound in Singapore by Tien Wah Press.

10   9   8   7   6   5   4   3   2   1

British Library Cataloguing in Publication Data available.
ISBN 978 1 84270 756 2
This book has been printed on acid-free paper

The Story Blanket

FERIDA WOLFF • HARRIET MAY SAVITZ

Illustrated by ELENA ODRIOZOLA

Andersen Press • London

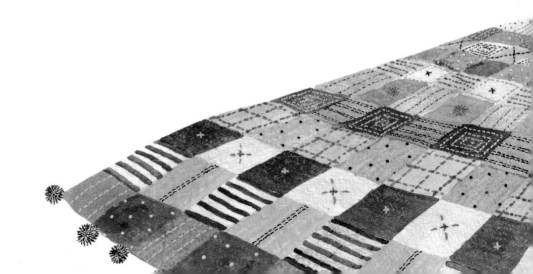

Deep in the snow-covered mountains, was the tiny village where Babba Zarrah lived. The children loved to settle down on Babba Zarrah's big old story blanket to listen to her stories.

One day Babba Zarrah noticed there was a hole in Nikolai's shoe. When the children left, she decided to knit Nikolai some nice, warm socks. But so much snow had fallen that winter that no one could get through to the village to deliver wool. How could she knit socks without wool?

"Every question has an answer," said Babba Zarrah. "I just have to think of it."

She poured herself a glass of sweet tea to help her think. Before she had taken three sips, Babba Zarrah knew what to do.

"I will unravel a little of the story blanket and use the wool for Nikolai's socks!" she said.

Late at night when everyone
was asleep, Babba Zarrah trekked
through the snow and left the
socks on Nikolai's doorstep.

Soon after, the postman found a scarf
wrapped around his mailbag when he left
to start his morning rounds.

"Do you know who made it?" he asked
everyone he met.

But no one did.

The schoolmaster was surprised to
find a pair of warm mittens on the
woodpile when he brought in wood for
the school stove.

Mrs Ivanov flapped the ravens from
her wash with the new knitted apron she
discovered beside her water pump.

Before long, the grocer was wearing a new shawl instead of the moth-eaten one she used to have.

The children had to sit closer on the blanket when they came for a story.

Day by day, the villagers grew more curious.

Baby Olga received a mysterious new soft blanket, and the butcher showed off the fancy woollen cap that covered his shiny bald head.

The children were now squashed together on the very small story blanket.

The confusion grew when the tailor's
scraggly cat suddenly showed up, purring
and grand, in a snug cat coat.

There was no blanket left to sit on.

The villagers asked the mayor to help them solve the mystery.

"You know what Babba Zarrah always says," the mayor replied. "Every question has an answer."

When the children saw the socks, the scarf, the mittens, the apron, the shawl, the cap, the baby blanket and the cat in her coat all together, they shouted, "It looks like Babba Zarrah's old story blanket!"

"But she doesn't have it any more," said Nikolai.

"Aha," said the mayor. "Babba Zarrah used the wool in her blanket to make these.

Now it's our turn to give Babba Zarrah a surprise."

So while Babba Zarrah slept, a few rows of wool were unravelled from every blanket in every household and left on Babba Zarrah's doorstep.

Babba Zarrah was amazed when she opened her front door in the morning. She had never seen so much wool, in so many colours. And on top of it all was a sign:

For Your New Story Blanket

The next time the
children went to Babba
Zarrah's for a story, there
was a colourful new blanket to sit on
and a tale about a village where everyone
shared with each other.

As she hugged the children goodbye,
Babba Zarrah noticed a hole in Alexandra's
sweater. She wanted to knit Alexandra a
surprise but the snow was still on the hills
and no wool was to be had anywhere in the
village.

Babba Zarrah knew that every question
had an answer. She looked at her new story
blanket and smiled.

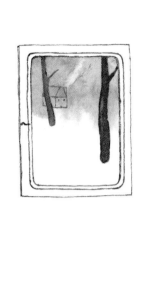

Also illustrated by Elena Odriozola
THE OPPOSITE